Woody Vanilla and Berry Truffle

*A guide on how to – or how
not to – deal with love.*

Chanda Abijah

Woody Vanilla and Berry Truffle

I dedicate this book to you. To your healing.

To your restoration. To your growth. To your story.

One of hope. Where beauty turns into ashes.

Where mourning becomes joy. Where tears become smiles.

I dedicate this book to you.

Overcomer.

CONTENTS

Chapter One:
Glimpses into the past

A WRITER'S HEART

We speak about the blooming and blossoming.
We speak about the sun rising, the moons lightening and the stars shining.
We speak about the sun kissing our skin, our hearts deeply intertwined with the pen, skillfully wrought into the firmament of our tongues. Forming words, rhymes, melodies. From deep within.

<u>A writer's heart.</u>
We speak about the tornadoes. The storms. Hope dying, souls crying, hearts aching and foundations shaking.

<u>A writer's heart.</u>
The epitome of the issues of life, love, peace, war, unity, hatred. All of this wrapped in the ABC's, the 123's, the anecdotes, the antidotes, the lover's soul.

<u>A writer's heart.</u>
More than just a place where words begin to make sense or none at all.
More than just a place where rhymes align, their sounds so sweet, it goes down like a honeycomb, sweet and fine.
More than just a place where the pen meets the paper.

<u>A writer's heart.</u>
Where the soul, mind and heart are stirred by themes so noble, only Kings and Queens are deserving.
Deserving to see, to read, to be. Anything, everything, everywhere at any given time.

<u>A writer's heart.</u>
Where words become poetry. Poetry becomes art and art becomes <u>freedom.</u>

SHY

"She is shy".

They used to say. So, as they labelled me, my mind kept drifting away.

"She is shy".

They used to say. As I envisioned myself on the greatest stage.

"She is shy".

They used to say.

So, after a while my lips got used to staying close to each other.

It is easier not to explain.

It is easier to dream in silence.

Speak in silence.

Exist in silence.

Suffer in silence.

WHAT 2PAC AND I HAD IN COMMON

"Is life worth living should I blast myself?"
At age nine maybe ten, I didn't have a gun as weapon. So, I had to
find something else strong enough to "blast myself".

Suicide.

It's real. The voice that tells you, you're not worth it. Is real. The
voice that tells you no one loves you. Is real. The voice that makes
you feel like you don't belong. Is real.

I remembered a movie I saw. A beautiful woman in her bathtub.
Sobbing. As she stood up to plug in the hairdryer. She turned it on
and I asked myself: "What is she trying to do?"
The water kept running, her tears kept falling, as she lowered the
blow dryer and dropped it into the bathtub she was lying in, covered
in water.
I remember wondering how so quickly her face turned from pain to
ease as she decided to leave. This time for good.

Suicide.

I saw it and thought "This looks easy, this I can do." So, as I entered
the bathroom, locked the door behind me and started to let the water
run. I looked for the dryer my mum would use to dry my hair. I
found it. I plugged it in. 'Good for me!' The cable was just long
enough to reach the bathtub I was going to lie in.
Ready to take the last steps of my life.. someone knocked on the
door heavily.

"Chanda hurry up! I need to pee."

Quickly I unplugged the dryer. Quickly I let the water sink. Quickly my heart began pounding in normal pace again. Quickly I looked around. Seeing. Realizing. This wasn't a dream.
I heard the knocking again.
"Hurry up, man! I need to pee!"

Suicide.

What looked so easy on the TV screen, didn't feel half as good in real life. The ease I had assumed on her face. I later realized was a silent cry for help. One that wished she had had a brother annoying enough, to stop her from taking this decision. I looked at the water in the bathtub sinking, thinking to myself:

"If only also she had had a brother that had to pee."

PIECE OF ME

There were pieces of me that I didn't see. Pieces of me that I didn't want to see.

Pieces of me that were broken. Pieces of me left unspoken about.

It took His love and peace, to pick up carefully every broken piece and form it into poetry.

"And the Lord God formed [wo]man of the dust of the ground and breathed into [her] nostrils the breath of life; and [wo]man became a living being."

A piece of me. Woman.

HOW SOULS SPEAK

The expression of a deeply troubled soul can go two ways.

They scream, they are angry and frustrated. The world is fault and everything and everyone in it. They never wanted and they never deserved what happened to them. They were never loved enough. They were never heard. Frustration and darkness, thick clouds of black, cover their mind and their heart. One way.

The other way.

The expression of a deeply troubled soul. A contrite spirit. A broken heart. Finds a way. It gets hold of a pen. Dark ink running out of it looking like the state of their being. They get hold of paper.

White, pure, light, eternal.
They do the impossible. They try the unimaginable.
The pen hits the paper as the first letter is created. Their hand shaky and sweaty as they release pain inexplicable.
"F"

The first letter. Drops of sweat on their forehead as they feel something inside their belly turning.

"R"

Their hand is moving, their head is pounding. "Is this me?"

They ask themselves inwardly as their hands create the letters "E" and "E". They drop the pen. They stare at it.
They found the cure. The vaccine. The way to express the state of their deeply troubled soul. They found it in this, that they discovered the art of writing.

"F R E E".

MISERY

It is a misery when a girl's first heartbreak

Is from no other man but her father.

It is a misery because she learns that love equals disappointment.

She learns that love equals mistrust and misuse.

She learns that she isn't deserving of the most natural gift a father can gift his children with.

So, she begins to lover herself.

Wrong of course.

Because now it is the anger, hurt, the insecurity and brokenness that shape a silhouette.

So, as she begins to look into the mirror, the view is so cloudy, that she begins to think it fits.

She begins to believe that her beauty is the ugliness of anger. Her charming smile now the epitome of hurt. The beauty they once praised her for, she now feels insecure about. The heart that once felt loved, now scattered into pieces. And every time she tries to pick up one, she cuts herself. So, she decides to leave them on the floor. While bleeding.

A misery. Father issues.

WHAT IF..?

What if, she was so busy, stressed and burned out because, not only was she "Mummy" but she was "Daddy" too?

What if, she never had the time to come to performances, plays and parent-teacher conferences because, if she had, it would have meant that you'd have to go without food the next day?

What if, she loved you, but never told you, because she didn't know that your love language was words of affirmation whilst hers was acts of service?

What if, she cried herself to sleep almost every night, praying and hoping that God would grant her mercy?

What, if she tried her best?

What if, Mama had known that she could have left him, and still be a woman and mother worthy of her call?

What if, she had known that her feelings mattered?

What if, Mama had known that a man, a real man, doesn't only bring money home but cares for his family too?

Reminiscing.

TRAPPED

The urging desire to please Him

mixed in the confusion

of the urging desire to please herself.

"They didn't care"

"They didn't love me"

so, she learned to "love" herself.

She was confused, it felt so good

but it didn't last longer than 10 seconds.

"Is this the love everybody talks about?"

"Is this the love they boast of so proud?"

Confused she looks into the mirror.

"Lust or Love?"

Trapped.

THE ABSENT FATHER

It wasn't you or anything you have done that made him run.

It was the absent father.

The one that never learned,

the one that never knew,

the one that didn't think he could.

So, when he saw your precious face,

the bright future ahead of you

He got scared thinking; he doesn't want to hurt you.

He never learned how to take care of gold,

and if he starts now, and then eventually gets it,

he might be too old.

So, he knew not but to run.

Away.

Because that is all he has ever seen.

Absence.

"As you are dealing with your father issues, allow your father to deal with his".

BLEEDING ROSES

She held roses in her hands.

She was smiling.

Seemingly happy.

So focused on her outward beauty that they didn't see she needed help.

The thorns were stinging.

She was bleeding.

But nobody was focused on that.

Because she held roses in her hands.

And she was smiling.

THE POWER OF TEARS

It wasn't the fact that I did not want to be healed. It wasn't the fact that I liked the state I was in. But as I saw the millions of broken pieces inside of me, it reminded me of the stars. Uncountable, innumerable pieces of me, shattered on the floor. The stars have lost their power to shine and fly. Rejection, abandonment, and lack of selflove were their kryptonite.

I didn't know who to speak to. I didn't know what to say. So, as I was asking myself what to do next, I heard a small voice within me whispering

"Pray".

"Pray!?" I thought to myself. I hated the one that created me. I hated the one that thought it was a good idea to place me in this world. I can't speak to Him. I cussed Him out. Said things I am too ashamed to bring back to my memory. He will not listen to me.

As tears were streaming down my face. My thoughts were catapulting me to another space. I heard it louder than I did before.

"Pray".

I couldn't.

I couldn't say a word. But my tears. They did. They were speaking the language I had in the split of a second unlearned to speak.

They were screaming, lamenting, questioning, repenting all on behalf of me. On behalf of my doubt, my sin and unbelief. I couldn't believe my ears as I heard the voice inside of me pleading for forgiveness. And I couldn't believe myself as I wept uncontrollably, feeling lighter with every tear that dropped out of me. As if they were unloading the burden, I kept inside of me for so long.

When I couldn't speak, my tears spoke for me.

SCATTERED PIECES

Even in the breaking there is beauty.

Scattered pieces are art too.

THROUGH THE EYES OF GOD

"If only you could see yourself

as I the Lord am seeing you,

you'd finally understand

that no brand of make up

can enhance,

what I have carefully mend together.

You would finally see and understand,

that it is not the beard that makes you a handsome man.

It is me in You.

It is You in me.

In my image I created you to see what I see,

When I look at you.

I see me."

Imago Dei. Made in the image of God.

CHURCH SERVICE

"When are we going to meet again?" He asked.

"Soon." She replied.

And she couldn't stop smiling.

"Why did no one tell me that this thing can feel so good? Why did no one care to share this simple secret with me?"

She thought, when she began to unleash the fear, the anxiety, the trauma. When she began to walk into the unknown that felt so peaceful and real. Almost as if anything else she's experienced before was a scam.

"It does exist!" She thought.

"It is real." She said, grinding as she walked down the street to get back home.

"Oh, had I known!" She exclaimed, sighing relieved.

"Oh, had I known, that He was the best thing that could ever happen to me. Oh, had I known that real love, true love, peaceful love, it exists."

"Hey honey! How did it go?" Her mother asked when she stepped inside the house.

"Mum? He is awesome!"

As she approached her daughter to hug her, she cried. But this time they were tears of joy.

"Didn't I tell you, honey, that if you allow Him to show himself to you, He will do so?"

As they hugged, tears running down their faces, their hearts were smiling and

Their heartbeats were humming the song:

"True love! Finally, they found you."

"Let's sit down and talk" Her mum said, when they finally let go off each other.

"Come on baby girl! Tell me how the church service went."

Chapter Two:
Love and his companions

A DEFINITION OF 'LOVE'

To love is not merely an emotion.

To love is a conscious decision of unveiling, unmasking, and unclothing.

Not the face, nor the clothes of your body.

But the soul, the self, the spirit.

Let's get naked.

LOST

I'm scared that I'll wake up someday and regret the day I fell in love with him.

There is something in his eyes that looks like death.

Something that cuts off my breath.

Yet, when I look at him, I see something I always wanted.

A man that loves a woman.

Yes, he screams sometimes.

Yes, he punches.

Love is not easy.

He's what I wanted.

Now what I got.

I'm scared that I'll wake up someday and regret the day I fell in love with him.

I'm awakening.

I'm lost.

TWISTED LOVE

He promised that he'll take care of her

So, as he began to unclothe her.

She began to surrender.

Quietly.

She thought sex was love.

So, she let him do what she thought lovers were supposed to.

How was she supposed to know that, what felt and tasted so good,

was only but a vapor of breath.

A moaning a groaning.

He finished.

He left.

Now she sat on the bed thinking: "If that was love why am I sitting here alone again?"

Still desperately wanting to be wanted.

Wanting to be.

Loved.

Sex. Twisted - When understood as love.

DECOMPOSING SYLLABLES

We.

As each letter put together forms a word, a sentence, a new meaning.

We did too.

You were the sense to my meaning and the synonym to every beautiful word there is.

As time passed on and seasons changed, and I began unmasking the layers of my heart. As I began to look deep within, I thought.

We were it.

The love songs, the butterflies, the feeling high without feeling doomed. The drug that caused all of this was love.

Love, we thought.

We.

Did not see that love that was supposed to be free, cost us.

All we had.

So, we.

Had to sit back, declutter, and unpack. Check the bags of our past relationships and all the ships of life we sailed on, packing and unpacking bags of experiences, life lessons, and traumas.

We.

Packed and unpacked so much that sometimes, in a hurry to rush to a new destination, we forgot to get rid of the former pain, resentment, bitterness and unforgiveness we had collected in our bags.

We were relentless.

Hopelessly carrying burden over burden into this thing called friendship. While these ships were sinking, we were thinking, we found love.

Now.

I am decomposing the syllables. The letters, the words, the rhymes, the songs, the butterflies, the laughter, the sweet silliness of it all.

Seemingly obvious it has become that in seeing, we were blind.

In hearing, we were deaf.

We didn't see.

We didn't see.

That loving us was costly. It cost us you. It cost us me.

It is now 'you' and 'me'. Now there is no longer 'w   e'.

~Decomposing syllables.

NO MORE

Apparently, she wasn't good enough.

Apparently, he was.

So anytime he broke her heart..

"It's deserved, it's my fault."

She thought.

Looking back now, she sees the lies.

The hurt.

The betrayal, the pain.

Not hers, but his.

And she realizes there is no reason for her to be ashamed.

His brokenness made her understand that people go through things.

Undeserved, unwillingly, it hurts, it cuts, it stings.

Yet all of that does not take from the fact that He had no right,

nor will he ever have

to break her heart like that.

Ever.

Again.

CATER 2 U

I loved you because you catered to my broken soul.

Now I love myself.

And since then the love for you has vanished.

LOVE'S CLAWS

I thought it was love, when in reality I had found another one.

Another one trying to put back together the broken pieces,

breaking them even more because he had claws, not hands.

A circle of mistakes repeated in this, that her weakness were men weaker than her.

He should have been her hero.

He should have eased the pain.

He should have taken care of her.

He should have taken away the shame.

As the tables were turning and the roles were shifting, she realized it. What they had in common wasn't love.

It was brokenness.

When the hand that was supposed to hold you turns into the hand that suffocates you -

It's Love's claws.

RECLAMATION

You remember what you gave to me

but hardly ever what you took from me.

My dignity

My strength

My love

My heart

My smile

My faith

I'm taking it back!

No longer do you hold the key to my freedom in your hand

No longer do you hold.

Me.

THE DAY STRANGERS BECAME LOVERS

We were doing what lovers were supposed to.

"And how was that an issue?"

The issue was that we weren't supposed to be lovers. We were strangers drawn together by the same weaknesses, brokenness, and insecurities.

We weren't in love.

We were fillers. Trying to heap in water into vases and didn't see they had holes in them. It didn't matter how hard we tried to fill each other's voids. It wasn't going to work. We missed the fact that what we lacked couldn't be found in neither of us.

The only one that could give to us, what we were so deeply looking for was the one we shut out.

God.

So, the moment I stopped heaping buckets of the little water I had left in me, into you. You could easily move on to another one.

Cause what we had wasn't love and it wasn't friendship.

What we had was a silent contract of two strangers suffering together in silence. Allowing demons and oceans of emotions to lead us into thinking we could do this together not realizing we were sinking.

Deep.

The water we kept heaping into each other, who would have thought that this would become the water we would later drown in?

We were trying to help us, but we didn't see we were killing us.

Slowly, softly, gently, and quietly.

We were drowning in the sea of hopelessness, hoping we could hold on to each other's traumas, thinking they would be the safety net.

Not knowing they were the trigger and reason our ocean became bigger and deeper each time we met.

The day strangers became lovers is the day you and I allowed ourselves to be misled.

WHAT'S LOVE GOT TO DO WITH IT?

I hated love. Because of him, because of her.

I hated love because of what they made of it.

Emptiness.

Lies.

Betrayal.

Hurt.

Fists in faces.

Confusion.

Pain.

Words that leave traces. Traces of blood.

But then He came.

In shape and form of a man. With deeds so upright only goodness could survive looking at him. Yet because of the evilness in people's heart they didn't see that the star that shined so bright was now in front of them.

He became human. With actions that speak louder than words, he humbled himself, came to serve on this earth.

He lived, he healed, he delivered, he cried, he worshiped, he smiled. He transformed. He forgave. He didn't love. He was love. He is love. Jesus.

With him I got to realize that what I believed was a lie. What I saw was never love. What I experienced was never from God.

Mere emotions mixed with the thought of love, so complex to put into words, so they turned it into hurt. Not knowing that words are not enough to describe the love that gave me,

Them.

Us.

Life.

Jesus.

THE SIGNATURE OF GOD

HE asked her best friend whether the news was true.

"She's engaged?"

"Yup!" she replied.

"Oh, wow!" HE answered.

"Lol! Is this a happy or a sad wow?" She asked jokingly wondering why HE'd asked in the first place.

HE didn't text her back.

<u>Wedding day</u>

On the day of her wedding, as she walked down the aisle her eyes searched every face until her eyes and HIS eyes locked. HE nodded, half smiling, half downcast. She quickly fixed her gaze on her future again. Seeing a blurry view of the man she chose to be with in the end. The man that saw her and thought she was a good woman. He saw her serve and minister in church and knew this is what he wanted. He was a good man. He loved her. He had a good heart. But she never really had peace about him. It just didn't spark.

<u>The wait</u>

As the years passed by her hope began to fail. She thought to herself, maybe after all it wasn't God. "I thought our souls connected when we first spoke. I thought the stars in heaven aligned when we began to sink into conversation about life, growth, God, and love. I thought that this was it. I thought I had finally found love. And I waited and waited, waking up every morning to check, if the day was the day. The day where HE would text me and say HE felt it too. HE saw it too. HE knew it too."

She waited. Days, weeks, months, years. The text never came. The phone never rang. The conversations began to cease. Estranged she would look at his profile picture. Hurt, she was at the thought of this being nothing but her imagination. Her heart had tricked her.

Never in her life has she ever felt this way and now only to find out that her heart was a trickster. And a good one too.

<u>Wedding day</u>

So as she walked down the aisle to approach the man that had approached her, taken her out on dates, assuring her daily that she was a beautiful, loving, kind woman, she could not but think: "What if I had waited a bit longer?" "What if I had asked HIM?" "What if I had called HIM?"

The "what if's" continued until she stood in front of him. The other him. The one that didn't take too long in knowing whether he liked her or not. The one that asked her out on dates she would have wished HE would've asked her out on.

The veil was covering her face as she took her eyes off him to look at HIM. HE didn't look back. HIS face was facing the floor. As she turned to look at her future husband to be, tears were rolling down her cheek. She tried to force a smile at him wondering, if he ever felt the distance between them? Her absence in mind when they were talking? Her serious face when he was smiling, whilst she was thinking, wondering what the other HE was doing at the moment.

<u>HE</u>

"God, help me to get through this day. Father I feel like watching my whole life passing me by, by watching the woman I thought you had for me marry someone else. I don't know if I can take this, so I ask you to help me right now."

HE prayed. As HE faced the floor trying to withhold tears.

"All these years, I was trying to become a better man, save money, work out, eat healthy, thinking about how I could provide a good future for her. And she walks down the aisle to someone that is not me?"

HIS mind was roaring. It seemed like the thoughts were beginning to scream so loud HE didn't hear the Pastor asking the congregation to sit down. It took him a moment to realize that HE was the only one in the church still standing, facing the floor.

"I can't do this Lord! What have I done wrong? I was working on me, for her. For us. What have I done wrong?"

HE finally sat down. HE could care less about the stares of people silently pleading for him to sit down. HE was about to watch the woman of his dreams marry someone that wasn't HIM. The dreams, the visions, the confirmations.

"So, all of this was a lie God!? EVERYTHING WAS A LIE?"

God

"When I made the heavens when I formed the earth, where was thou, o Man? When I spoke the light into existence and formed you of the dust of the earth, were you not as clay in my hands, o son of mine? You prayed, you served, yes, you love me. You are faithful, a man of valor and dignity. I promised you that if you can wait on me, I will not withhold anything good from you. I am not a man that I should lie, nor the son of man that I should repent. I withheld nothing good from you. Not even my precious daughter. I allowed your souls to recognize each other. I allowed your spirits to connect. My shalom I spoke over you two, but you've allowed the worries of this world and fear to lead you, instead of allowing me to. I told you provision comes from me. You said 'Lord, I got this.'

I said patience comes from me my daughter. You answered 'Lord, I have waited long enough. That's it.' So, as you both decided in your heart to not make me part of the beautiful story I, the Lord, was going to write. I had to allow you and let you go. As I cried looking at the hearts, I had destined to become one, fall apart with each and every step of own decision making, led by the standard of this world, neglecting the fact that this. This story. Was one where I wanted the world to see my Glory. My standard. My will be done. Perfected in the love of you my daughter. You, my son.

So, the next time you want to ask 'why'. Ask yourself why you couldn't trust me enough to perform what I had said I will. My words never come back to me empty, they never return void. You didn't even allow my word to grow. The seed of love to take root. You began to uproot before I could plant. And this. This is the result of it. A faith-based decision. Turned into a battle between fear and unbelief. You've left faith out. And with that you've blotted me out. The story that was about to have my signature on the wedding certificate, now has yours on it.

- You decided to write the story only I could have written.

That's the very reason your hearts are broken. "

Bitter. Sweet. Love.

Chapter three:

Changing the narrative

BORROWED LOVE

The areas of our hearts, that we so strongly occupy with disappointment, unforgiveness, brokenness, pain, frustration, and anger, is nothing but wasted capacity that we could use to love someone that really needs it. Someone that wishes there were someone that would open up a little space of the comfort of their hearts for them to sit in it and experience warmth, in the place they are used to living in a cold world.

When close to us, let's allow people to feel the love of God embracing them, when we reach out for a hug.

When close to us, let's allow people to feel the warmth of peace surrounding them when we enter their presence.

Let's lend them a piece of our love. Even if they are not able to pay us back, they might be able to lend that piece of love to someone else that is in need of it too.

Create a chain reaction.

A chain reaction of love being passed down.

Borrowed love is generational wealth.

THE SHIFTING

I saw dark clouds, storms, and thunder.

Rain falling in masses.

As I continued worshiping the heavens released even more rain.

I closed my eyes and concentrated on Him.

I didn't look at the clouds anymore, didn't concentrate on the storms, didn't listen to the sound of the thunder.

It became quiet. In my heart I began to feel peace.

"Did the storm stop?"

No.

"Did the rain stop pouring?"

No.

"Did the thunder stop roaring?"

It didn't.

But what happened was that my focus shifted from my problems to the ultimate problem solver.

God.

"Peace be still".

MY VOWS – IN A MAN'S ARMS

I never felt safe in a man's arms. I never felt secure. I never felt wanted. I never felt needed. A man's arms reminded me of betrayal. Of rejection. Of violence. Of hurt. Of pain.

In his arms.

In his arms for the first time I feel loved. I feel secured. I feel wanted. I feel needed. His hug is as firm as the wall of Jericho that, if I wanted, only praise and worship could tear down. His kiss on my forehead feels like the early dew resting gently and humbly on the grass of the fields.

His love. Had I known earlier what I would experience, I would have waited more patiently, more willingly, more joyfully. This gentle, patient, kind, peace-loving and selfless King.

The one I love to see seated next to me, as we sit on our thrones watching our legacy bear the fruit that we have so carefully tended, guarded, preserved, protected.

The one that makes my heart skip beats every time he looks at me. His smile gives me assurance. His laughter gives me peace. His protection makes me understand his love.

For me.

So, as I unfold myself, carefully. As I bloom into becoming. As I rise like the cedars of Lebanon. My prayer is that I will be everything you need me to be and more. I pray that I will reflect the peace of Jesus in the midst of the storm. The love of Jesus in the midst of trials. And the joy of Jesus in the midst of turbulence.

I pray that I will never cease to see the joy, love, peace, and happiness that God brought me when He brought me You.

In your arms – I feel at home.

A FAITHFUL ONE

When you smiled at me, I felt the peace of God hugging me. Assuring me. Caressing me. Telling me. That it will be well.

"Because you have trusted me. This time around I am sending a faithful one".

SAFE H[E]AVEN

And when nothing else seems to make sense,

I'll run to you my safe haven.

Because when I am with you,

it feels like I'm in heaven.

THE ONE

When I'm around you,

I feel a peace that is so tangible that it scares me.

You are

The one.

WHIRLWINDS AND TORNADOES OF LOVE

Intertwined in the whirlwind of two worlds,

tossed to and fro by the tornados of love.

I knew it.

It was you.

Because when I looked into the beauty of your eyes.

I saw me.

Happy.

Free.

Loved.

Alive.

In your eyes I saw it. For the first time. It hit me.

The wind uplifted me.

The tornado shifted me.

The whirlwind dropped me,

back in front of you.

It was you.

I'm in Love.

REFLECTION

I thought I knew you.

The way you spoke was familiar.

The way you helped, loved, prayed, and served reminded me of someone I had heard of.

So, I did my research.

You are not as perfect as He is.

But you are trying to be.

So, as I took some time I remembered.

You reminded me of Him.

Jesus.

Reflection.

THE TURTLE AND THE DOVE

"If a turtle and a dove fall in love, where are they going to build a house?"

"In the sky" I thought. "The highest part of it too!"

I am the turtle, bound to the earth and the mud of this world. You are the dove. Seeing you makes me believe in the fact that

With you

I can be anything I want to be.

With you

I can fly. I can be anywhere I want to be. So, I choose the skies.

A housing, free of judgment and prejudice. A place where color of skin and age don't take away from the heart of gold within.

Precious.

This love is precious to me.

I'll cross the hottest desert, crawl on my knees, swim through the red sea, so that your beautiful face, I can see.

If a turtle and a dove fall in love, their hearts, yes, their hearts will be each other's resting place.

And on it. On the ground of two hearts becoming one, love shining on them like the light of the sun.

They build. Not a house. But a home - their safe place.

HOME

As the star has its home in the skies.

So, I want you to have your home in my heart.

EASY LOVIN'

You make loving you easy.

It seems like a natural gift. Like me breathing without thinking twice about it. As if in my mother's womb, when God was knitting together the parts of my body and formed my heart, He had you in mind placing you in the middle right from the start.

You make loving you easy.

As a walk on the beach or in the park. Every time I look at you, I feel a spark. I am reminded of the love of God, His patience, His kindness, His goodness, His love, His peace.
You make loving you easy.

It feels like a breeze of fresh and cold air on a hot summer day. Like the ice cubes in a sparkling coke with fresh lemon on top.

Love.

It isn't the emotions or butterflies that keep me at an all-time high or me wanting to be present and active in the here and now with you.

Love.

It is the continuous assurance that this life, I don't want to walk with anyone else by my side but you.

Because You make loving you easy.

Chapter Four:
Stepping into healing

COLORFUL DRESSES AND THE TIME OF HIS VISITATION

I saw them coming in every week. Looking gorgeous in their colorful dresses, their beautiful handbags matching the colors of their new pair of shoes. Shoes they would only wear on Sundays. Dresses they would only iron on Sundays. Handbags that were only good enough for Sundays. What I saw beyond that were little children stuck in the bodies of now adult men and women. Men and women who were taught that religion was merely measured by acting right, doing right, being right. An act strictly monitored by the eyes of people that were ready to cage every ounce of freedom and exploratory willingness.

A willingness to look beyond the letters, read between the lines. A willingness to stop following the masses for a second and refocus on the Master.

The true one.

The real one.

Unlike popular beliefs it wasn't the one driving in every week in the fanciest car, wearing the most expensive clothes or having the most beautiful woman on his side.

It was the one coming in every Sunday. Wearing the same ripped shirt, that once was white and over time had turned into ash grey. The one that no one cared to ask, why He always wore the same clothes every Sunday. Why he always smelled like he never took showers. Why he could not stop crying every Sunday, whilst people were enjoying the ear tickling messages of the Pastor. The one that would stand at the door speaking to himself an hour before they would start service. The one that no matter what season, spring, summer, autumn, winter, would come in the ripped shirt, raggedy jeans and torn slippers.

They didn't know that as they were inside the temple praising, praying, worshipping. Giving, smiling, laughing. He was at the altar crying, asking, pleading. That God would open their eyes so they could recognize Him.

That God would have mercy on them just one more week so He could save them. That God would grant Him more time so He could reveal himself once more.

They had eyes, but they were blinded. Had ears but were deaf. Their praises were empty just as their hearts were empty. They were blinded by all the splendor of the world and forgot the creator of it. Were struck by all the ways it made their flesh feel that they forgot that of dust they were formed and to dust they shall return.

One day He came back, early, to pray as He did for them every day. Just to read a note on the door of the entry to the church reading

"Hey you! We don't know your name, but we know you will come as you always do. We changed location. We are growing so much that we bought a new Arena. It is an hour's drive from here and since we know you can't make it, we left you an envelope. Use the money to buy yourself something to eat and don't be sad. You will find a new church to worship in. Maybe one that is closer to where you stay?"
- Blessings, The Church

"Now as He drew near, He saw the city and wept over it, saying, "If you had known, even you, especially in this your day, the things that make for your peace! But now they are hidden from your eyes. For days will come upon you when your enemies will build an embankment around you, surround you and close you in on every side, and level you, and your children within you, to the ground; and they will not leave in you one stone upon another, because you did not know the time of your visitation".

SKIN DEEP

He began to unveil the layers of skin that were like the walls of Jericho.

THICK. DEFENSIVE. SECURED. ANCHORED.

Anchored in pain, that He was willing to heal.

Secured in anger, that He was willing to turn into songs of joy.

Defensively she was trying to uphold the walls that seemed to start crumbling.

Thick she thought they were. Until The Wall Breaker came.

Layer per layer.

He took it away.

The shame.

The rejection.

The pain.

Skin deep.

THE QUEEN'S MISTAKE

I see a strong, beautiful, black woman.

I see an independent queen.

I see a warrior.

I see a fighter.

I see a lover.

I see a giver.

I see a strong, beautiful, black woman.

I see people scared.

They see a strong, beautiful, black woman and they get scared. They see the power that lies in the way that she carries herself and they are worried. Their insecurities now lay bare before them and instead of learning from the strong, beautiful, black woman they decide to cage her. They decide to belittle her. They decide to make her feel like the brown gold she is covered in is dirt. Like the kinky curls she wears as a crown is rubbish.

And so, she begins to crumble apart.

I see a strong, beautiful, black woman now trying to be everything and everyone but her beautiful self.

Now I see a strong, beautiful, black woman. Confused. Because she looks in the mirror and now no longer sees what she once thought was beautiful. She looks at her skin and is disgusted. She looks at her hair and is disturbed. The crown she once carried with dignity and grace has become a heavy burden. The skin that seemed like the purest covering of gold, now itchy and sticky.

Not because she was brought up to think that way.

But because she was told a lie.

She was told she was ugly and the biggest mistake she ever made was to believe the lie.

WHO CAN HEAL ME?

".. and, if it feels like your wound is as deep as the sea and you ask yourself

'Who can heal me?'

I dare you to open your eyes and see me.

Hanging on the cross, nail per nail I'll take it away.

The hurt, the memory, the rejection, the shame, the pain.

As I did in ancient days, I'll do again for you.

I'll part the red sea. I'll quiet the storms. I'll speak to the winds.

Just leave that to me.

Then you will see that the red sea is nothing to me.

But I care about your wounds.

I'll bind them for you.

I promise my child, that if you'll trust me.

I will take care of you.

'My wound is as deep as the sea, who can heal me?'

I, alpha and Omega. I, Jehovah-Rapha. Your Healer."

THE VALLEY OF THE SHADOW OF DEATH

As she walked through the valley of the shadow of death, she began to remember that David said: "In that place, fear no evil!".

So, she kept on walking.

Through the tears.

Through the pain.

Until she got there.

In his shadow she found rest.

Now she was saved because she found the secret place.

~ Psalm 91

LOVE'S LOVE

Let love love you

like the father that tried

yet couldn't,

because he never had a father

that showed him how he should have

loved love.

HEALING'S HUG

Let healing hug you,

like the mother that never did,

because

she didn't know how to.

YOU

Healing is for you.

You deserve to be made whole again.

You deserve to be loved again.

Don't give them the power

to make you base your right to be loved

on their wrong.

THRIVING

In pain there are good days and bad days.

There are those when you feel like crying.

There are those where you can't stop smiling.

In both remember to keep going.

Keep thriving.

STREETS OF GOLD

Someone asked me:

"Why aren't you afraid of death?
I asked back:
"How can you be afraid of walking on gold for the rest of your life?"

Streets of gold.

No more mourning.

No more crying.

No more death.

No more pain.

Everlasting joy.

Everlasting glory.

Streets of gold, where the real walk of fame takes place. No pictures framed in the firmness of stone. But hearts fully surrendered and rooted in the firmness of Him, the corner stone.
Streets of gold diminish every fear there is. Because they remind me that I will walk straight into His arms. It's not the gold that makes it bearable and beautiful to me. It's the place these streets will lead me to.

Eternity spent with Jesus.

Where streets of gold become inane and life with Him reality.

Spending my life with Him.

For eternity.

EMOTIONAL SECURITY

I imagine walls breaking, rain falling and souls shaking.

I imagine darkness arising, thunder roaring and lightning striking.

It gets loud, I hear them screaming, crying, asking it to stop.

As we release the ugly demons that held us hostage in the prisons of hopelessness, brokenness, pain, and rejection.

As we release the fear of being hurt.

As we breath out anger and let out frustration.

The breaking begins to cease. Brick by brick I see rebuilding. Where there once was rain, I see sprouts, I see crops, I see new growth.

Where our souls were crying, I hear the sounds of joyful laughter.

As we successfully found the soul that was equally looking for a soul hungry for healing.

We found emotional security.

Not in the firm guarding of emotions ready to uncontrollably unleash the moment they are triggered.

Not in the swallowing and eating of the pills of pain we were fed by our circumstances.

We found emotional security.

By sharing.

By releasing.

By shouting.

By crying.

By believing.

By hoping.

By trusting.

By speaking.

By healing.

By singing.

By writing.

By finding.

The one that will open the door to his heart and allow us to take a seat in the place where the welcome sign reads:

"This is it. You have arrived in the King's chambers. The place of everlasting peace. Thank you for accepting the invitation into God's heart. Thank you for accepting healing".

POETRY

Poetry?

What's that to me?

Expression, Art, History.

Storytelling, being free.

No shackles, no hold, no boundaries.

Kissed by the sun, embraced in chocolate skin.

Perfection that lies deep within.

Mend together carefully, rooted in His love so deeply.

Poetry is not only when I sing

> is not only when I write
> is not only when I think

Poetry is not only when I smile

> is not only when I cry
> is not only when I see.

Poetry is not only within me. It is me. I am Poetry.

THE END AND THE BEGINNING

I am Poetry because the one who created me, did so knowingly.

Lovingly He formed me, so I can be part of his Poems to be. That the world might see, not me, but Him living through me.

I am telling a story of complexity. Of how a God so generously gave His only Son so compassionately, that I and you, so graciously.

May.

Be.

Free.

So, Poetry?

That's you. That's me.

"And now abide faith, hope, **love**, these three, but the greatest of these is **love**".

Printed in Great Britain
by Amazon

47794754R00043